For my cousin Helen, with love
~ C F

To my niece, Ella Victoria Wernert
~ T M

Copyright © 2007 by Good Books, Intercourse, PA 17534
International Standard Book Number: 978-1-56148-567-3; 1-56148-567-5

Library of Congress Catalog Card Number: 2006026165

Text copyright © Claire Freedman 2007
Illustrations copyright © Tina Macnaughton 2007

E
FRE

Original edition published in English by Little Tiger Press,
an imprint of Magi Publications, London, England, 2007.

Printed in China

Library of Congress Cataloging-in-Publication Data

Freedman, Claire.
One magical day / Claire Freedman ; [illustrations by] Tina Macnaughton.
p. cm.

Summary: From the dawn's first light to the full moon's gleam,
animals enjoy a wonderful summer day.
ISBN-13: 978-1-56148-567-3 (hardcover)
[1. Summer--Fiction. 2. Animals--Fiction. 3. Day--Fiction.
4. Stories in rhyme.] I. Macnaughton, Tina, ill. II. Title.
PZ8.3.F88On 2007
[E]--dc22
2006026165

One Magical Day

Claire Freedman   Tina Macnaughton

Intercourse, PA 17534
800/762-7171
www.GoodBks.com

Night shadows fade
to a pale, golden dawn.
It's a magical day –
wake up, Little Fawn!

Mother Duck wakens
her brood with a kiss.
This beautiful morning
is too good to miss!

Up in the poppy field
frisky lambs play,
Skipping with joy
on this new summer's day.

Small piglets scamper
and skip in the sun;
Rolling in mud
is such squelchy fun!

Warm breezes drift
down the flower-filled lanes,
Where fluffy-tailed puppies
run 'round, playing games.

Into the stable
the warm sunlight streams,
Bathing the foal
with its soft, golden beams.

Sun-drowsy kittens
pad home to their mother.
Washed one by one,
they curl up with each other.

Happy and free,
the wild swallow weaves,
Then swoops to her nest,
built high in the eaves.

Little calves rest
in the shade of the trees,
Where butterflies dance
on the fresh, gentle breeze.

Donkey nods off
in the last patch of sun.
Softly the light fades;
the day's almost done.

Blinking in wonder,
two shy fox cubs peep,
As deep in the meadow,
the long shadows creep.

Stars shine like diamonds,
the full moon gleams bright,
Gently Owl hoots –
it's a magical night!